Skipper to the Rescue

Come flutter by
Butterfly Meadow!

✽

Butterfly Meadow

Skipper to the Rescue

by Olivia Moss
illustrated by Helen Turner

SCHOLASTIC INC.

New York Toronto London Auckland Sydney
Mexico City New Delhi Hong Kong Buenos Aires

With special thanks to Sue Mongredien

To Tom Powell

ISBN-13: 978-0-545-05459-1
ISBN-10: 0-545-05459-1

12 11 10 9 8 7 6 5 4 3 2 1   8 9 10 11 12 13/0

Printed in the U.S.A.

First printing, October 2008

Contents

Butterfly Meadow

Skipper to the Rescue

CHAPTER ONE

New Furry Friends

Whoooooosh! The long grasses of Butterfly Meadow swayed in the wind. "I feel like flying high into the sky," Dazzle said to her friend Skipper as the breeze tugged at her yellow wings.

"Me, too," Skipper replied. "Let's go exploring!" She fluttered over to

Twinkle, a peacock butterfly, and
Mallow, a cabbage white, who were
perched on nearby flowers. "We're going
flying. Want to come?"

"Sure," Mallow agreed, wiggling her
antennae.

Twinkle looked up from admiring her
colorful wings. "Sounds like fun," she
said. "Let's go!"

The four friends took to the air,
sailing along on the breeze. "This is so
cool," Mallow cried breathlessly as the
wind carried them toward the forest.
"Wheeeeee!"

Dazzle was enjoying the ride, too. She
barely had to flap her wings! They were
soaring over the meadow. She gazed
down at the flowers below, watching

their bright heads bob and dance. "Hey," Dazzle said suddenly. "What are those white things?"

She pointed with her wing to where three furry creatures hopped in the grass. Dazzle hadn't been out of her cocoon for long, so she was still discovering new things every day.

Skipper peered down. "They're bunnies," she replied. "Baby rabbits. Aren't they cute?"

Dazzle was curious. "Be right back," she called to her friends and swooped down toward the bunnies. As she approached, Dazzle could see that they all had long, fluffy ears and white whiskers.

Dazzle landed gently on one of the bunnies' pink noses. "Hello," she said.

The bunny laughed. "That tickles!" it squealed. "What are you? You're not a bunny."

Dazzle smiled. "I'm a butterfly," she told the bunny. "Am I the first butterfly you've ever seen?"

"Yes, I think you must be," the bunny said. Then it sneezed, sending Dazzle up into the air. "*Ah-chooo!* Oops — sorry!"

"That's okay," Dazzle said. She glanced up. Skipper, Mallow, and Twinkle were small specks, high up in the sky. "I'd better go catch up with my friends. Bye!"

"Bye!" the bunnies chorused. Peeking back over her wing, Dazzle saw all of

the bunnies sitting up on their hind legs,
watching her go.

Dazzle raced to catch up with her
friends, who had already reached the
edge of the forest. She found them near
a tree.

"Dazzle," Mallow called. "Come and
play — we're dodging the sycamore
seeds."

The long green sycamore seeds fell
from the tree, twisting and turning as
they floated to the ground. Dazzle's
friends zipped all around them,
laughing. Skipper was particularly
good at darting in between the seeds,
swerving nimbly so she wouldn't
get hit.

Dazzle joined in. "This is fun!" she
cried, ducking and diving like her

friends. "I love the way the seeds spin around and around. They look almost like butterflies' wings!"

"Those little wings help the seeds float away from the tree," Twinkle explained. "They'll have a better chance of growing if they don't land right next to the mother tree's roots. Neat, huh?"

Just then, a stronger gust of

wind blew through the forest. Dazzle had to dive away from the tree to avoid the shower of seeds. Then she gazed around, floating in the air. Where had her friends gone?

Skipper's voice rang out from a beautiful black cherry tree brimming with white flowers. "Hey, you guys!" she called excitedly. "Come and see what I've found!"

CHAPTER TWO

An Exciting Discovery

Dazzle, Mallow, and Twinkle flew straight to the tree. "What did you find?" Twinkle asked, perching on a branch.

"Look," Skipper said softly, pointing with her wing.

Dazzle wasn't sure what Skipper was so excited about. All she could see was a

piece of dried leaf that was attached to a twig at both ends. It looked like the leaf had been folded to make a long, thin pocket.

"A leaf?" Dazzle asked, confused.

"That's not *just* a leaf," Skipper replied with a mysterious smile.

Mallow thoughtfully tipped her

head to one side. "Something to eat?"
she guessed.

"A gift for me?"
Twinkle wondered
hopefully, twirling
on one leg.

"No," said Skipper. "It's a caterpillar
sleeping bag."

Right away, Twinkle and Mallow
both cheered and flew loops in the air.

Dazzle didn't understand why they all
seemed so happy. "A caterpillar sleeping
bag?" she echoed.
She took a closer
look. It didn't look
like a cozy place to
sleep — it was just a
crumpled leaf.

"That's right,"

Skipper said. "There's something very special inside it — a baby butterfly!"

"Oh!" Dazzle exclaimed. "That's a cocoon? Wow!" She had only seen one cocoon before — her own! It had been all torn apart by the time she'd emerged. Dazzle tapped gently on the dried leaf. "Hey, Little Butterfly," she said softly. "Want to come out and play?"

The wind blew through the tree again, and the cocoon swung on its twig like a tiny brown flag.

"It doesn't work like that," Mallow said kindly to Dazzle. "Butterflies only come out when they're ready."

Twinkle had darted into a cluster of flower blossoms nearby and was sipping nectar. "Think of your first day as a

butterfly," she said, raising her head. "No one was waiting for you to come out, right?"

Dazzle thought back to how she'd struggled in the darkness. She could remember the way she'd burst from her cocoon into the light. The world had seemed so bright! Dazzle had been excited, but lonely and scared, too. "I think I'll wait for the butterfly to come out," she announced. "I'd like to be here to welcome it."

Twinkle finished her nectar and gazed up at the sky. "I think we should head back to Butterfly Meadow," she said. "A storm is coming."

"Let's play tag first," Skipper suggested. She tapped Mallow with her wing. "Tag — you're it!"

While her friends chased one another around the trees, Dazzle perched near the cocoon. "Hey, there," she said to it. "I wonder what kind of butterfly you'll be?"

But then she stopped talking. Something was twitching inside the cocoon! Was the new butterfly about to appear?

CHAPTER THREE

A Storm Brews

The cocoon wiggled and jiggled.
Something was happening in there!

"Hey!" Dazzle called to her friends.
"I think the new butterfly is ready to
come out."

Skipper, Mallow, and Twinkle
zoomed over, but now the cocoon wasn't
doing anything! A ladybug walking

along the branch stopped at the sight of
the butterflies clustered around. "What
are you all looking at?" the ladybug
asked in surprise.

"It's a cocoon," Dazzle replied. "I
thought it was about to hatch into a
butterfly, but . . ."

"It was probably just the wind making
it move," Twinkle guessed.

Skipper looked up at the sky. "That storm's getting closer," she said.

The ladybug gazed up, too. "It sure is," she said. "Time for me to take cover." She scuttled away, her shiny red wings bouncing from side to side.

Dazzle shook her head. "You know, I don't think it was the wind. I'm sure I saw it move —" The cocoon twitched again. "There! Did you see that?"

"I did," Skipper said. "It definitely moved."

"I saw it, too," Twinkle added, twirling in the air. "Oh, this is so exciting! I wonder if the new butterfly will be as pretty as me?"

The branches rattled and the whole
tree swayed in the wind. Dazzle shivered.
Dark gray clouds were rolling across the
sky, blocking the sun.

A bright white flash and a loud
cracking sound made them all jump.
Dazzle had never seen anything like this
before. "What's happening?" she asked,
frightened.

"There's going to be a thunderstorm,"
Skipper told her, glancing nervously at
the sky. "We need to take cover before it

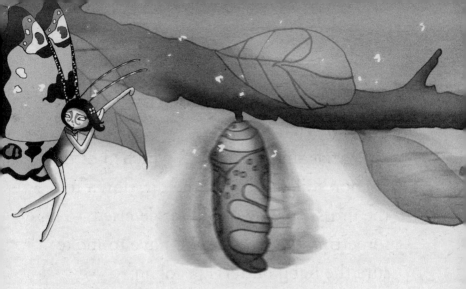

starts raining. If our wings get wet, we won't be able to fly home."

Dazzle's wings trembled as she and her friends ducked under a large branch. The wind whipped through the forest, making the trees groan and bend. Dazzle had enjoyed sailing on the breeze earlier, but now she was worried that it would blow her away!

Another fierce gust of wind tore through the trees. Leaves flew right off the branches. Oh, no! Dazzle saw a

large leaf knock the cocoon away from its twig.

Dazzle and her friends watched as the cocoon sailed through the air, down to the grass. "Come on!" Dazzle cried, forgetting the storm. "We have to make sure the baby butterfly is okay."

She and her friends struggled to fly down to where the cocoon had landed. No matter how hard Dazzle batted her wings, the wind kept trying to push her back.

Just as Dazzle was beginning to think it was hopeless, the wind stopped. She and her butterfly friends finally landed on the grass next to the cocoon. "How will the butterfly climb out safely during a thunderstorm?" Dazzle asked, frowning.

"We need to roll the cocoon to a place where it will be safe," Skipper decided. "Let's push it up against the tree trunk — it will be sheltered from the wind and rain there."

The four butterflies pushed hard. "Come on, team," Mallow called as they leaned against the cocoon. But it was no use. They weren't strong enough to move it.

The ladybug they'd met earlier flew overhead. "The storm's almost here," she called out. "You'd better go someplace dry."

Dazzle watched her go. An eerie silence filled the forest now.

"We need to get the cocoon under cover before the rain starts," Skipper said. "But how?"

CHAPTER FOUR

Go, Bunnies!

Dazzle suddenly had a great idea. "The bunnies might be able to help," she said.

Skipper clapped her wings together in excitement. "Good thinking, Dazzle! You and Mallow see if you can find them. Twinkle and I will stay here and guard the cocoon."

Dazzle nodded. "Don't come out until

I'm back," she whispered to the cocoon. Then she and Mallow fluttered through the gusting wind toward the meadow. "Imagine coming out into the world during a storm," she said to Mallow as they flew. "It would be so scary."

"Terrifying," Mallow agreed. "I hope those bunnies can help."

"There they are," Dazzle said, spotting three fuzzy white shapes bouncing in and out of a rabbit hole. "Let's go!"

"It's the flutter-flies again!" yelled the smallest bunny as

Dazzle and Mallow swooped down from the sky.

"No, it's the flutter-bys," a second bunny piped up.

"Hi, guys," Mallow said. "We're *butterflies*. And we need your help!"

She and Dazzle quickly explained what had happened to the cocoon. "Of course we'll help!" the smallest bunny said.

"We like you flutterbys," the second bunny added.

"It's butter — oh, never mind," Dazzle said. "This way — follow us!"

The two butterflies flew overhead while the bunnies bounced after them.

"The baby is definitely ready to hatch," Skipper told Dazzle as she

fluttered up to the tree. "Look, you can
see it vibrating inside."

Dazzle swooped down to peek.
Skipper was right! There was movement
under the papery surface of the cocoon.
Wow — a new butterfly was about to be
born!

"What should we do?" the smallest
bunny asked, bouncing up to the tree.

"Well," Skipper began, "I think the best place for the cocoon would be in the hollow over there, between the roots." She pointed her wing to a hole at the base of the tree. "Could you use your paws to gently nudge it there?"

"Sure!" the bunnies chorused, gathering around the cocoon.

The cocoon wriggled again.

It's almost as if the baby butterfly knows that the bunnies want to help, Dazzle thought.

The bunnies pushed at the cocoon with their soft paws. It bounced slowly along the ground. "Go, bunnies! Go, bunnies!" Mallow cheered.

"Keep it up!" Dazzle called out. She noticed that the other creatures in the forest were tucking themselves into safe

places before the storm. Hedgehogs were curling into tight balls, birds were flying to their nests, and all the crickets had fallen silent. She couldn't help but worry. Just how bad was this thunderstorm going to be?

The bunnies had almost nudged the cocoon to the hollow when a larger rabbit hopped up. Her whiskers twitched angrily.

"There you are!" she scolded the three bunnies. "I've been looking everywhere for you! Can't you feel that wind? A storm is coming. You need to get back to the burrow at once."

Dazzle flew down to explain. "They're just helping us push this cocoon to a safe place —" she began, but the mother rabbit wouldn't listen.

"And I need to get my babies to a safe place," she said curtly. "Come on, all of you. Hop to it!" "Yes, Mommy," the bunnies chorused. "Sorry," the smallest bunny whispered to the butterflies as they hopped away. Dazzle couldn't blame them for leaving. They had to listen to their mommy! She was only trying to keep them safe.

Another flash of bright light filled the air, followed by a loud rumble.

"The storm is getting closer," Twinkle said fearfully. "The thunder came right after the lightning — it's almost here!"

CHAPTER FIVE

Woof! Woof!

A loud bark rang through the air and the cocoon jerked, as if the noise had made it jump. Dazzle looked around, but she couldn't see a dog anywhere. "That's Buster," Mallow explained, seeing her friend's confused look. "He's the sheepdog that works in the field beyond those trees."

"That's it!" Skipper cried. "Buster's

good at herding sheep. I'm sure he could move one tiny cocoon! I'll go ask him right away."

"Me, too," Dazzle said. Glancing back at the cocoon, she followed Skipper to the field. A black-and-white dog was herding a flock of sheep into their shelter. Buster's ears were pricked, and his tail lashed the ground. Dazzle could tell that he was really concentrating!

She darted in front of Buster to get his
attention, but long, shaggy hair swung
in front of his eyes. "He can't see me,"
she called to Skipper.

"Let's both try," Skipper suggested.

The two butterflies danced before the
dog's face, but Buster suddenly bolted
after a sheep, and
they had to dive
out of the way.
One of the sheep
gazed up at Dazzle.
"He's only
interested in us,"
the sheep said
wearily. "He won't
stop until we're all safe in our shelter."

"Thanks," Dazzle said politely. There
had to be something they could do!

"I'll try getting closer," Skipper said. She flew as close to Buster's left ear as she could. "Buster! We need your —"

But her soft wings must have tickled Buster. He flapped his ears, as if he were trying to brush away a fly. Skipper had to quickly dodge out of the way.

"Woof! Woof!" Buster barked so loudly at the last sheep that Dazzle felt her wings shake.

"You take cover under the fence on the side of the field. It's going to rain any second," Skipper said. "It doesn't make sense for both of us to get caught in the rain."

"But —" Dazzle didn't want to leave her friend. "What will you do if the rain starts? Remember when Twinkle got her wings wet? She couldn't fly."

"I'll be okay," Skipper told her bravely. "I was good at dodging the sycamore seeds, wasn't I? I'll dodge the raindrops, too, if I need to. Now, go!"

CHAPTER SIX

Skipper Steps In

As Skipper fluttered back toward Buster, Dazzle flew beneath the fence. The sky was darker than ever. It was all up to Skipper now.

Skipper flew behind Buster as he herded the last sheep into the shelter. "That's it, ladies. Keep moving!" he barked. As one of the biggest sheep was trotting in, Skipper began flying in large circles above its head. The sheep craned its neck back to watch Skipper zoom around and around. The sheep's head turned in circles as it tried to watch what Skipper would do next.

Buster barked impatiently. "Come along!" he said to the sheep. "No stragglers, please." But the sheep

wouldn't move, even though fat drops of rain were starting to fall from the sky.

"What a beautiful butterfly!" Dazzle heard the sheep cry out. Buster glanced up at last! He saw Skipper circling in the air and shook the shaggy fur from his eyes for a better look.

"Well, I never," he said loudly.

Dazzle gave a cheer. Skipper did it! Now she just had to persuade Buster to help move the cocoon. Dazzle could see the little blue butterfly hovering by Buster's ear, and guessed that Skipper was telling the dog what had happened.

Buster ran toward Dazzle, with Skipper flitting above his head.

"Yay!" Dazzle cheered, as the dog jumped through a gap in the fence.

"He's going to try and help," Skipper

said, sounding relieved. "Nobody can round up animals like Buster!"

Back in the forest, heavy raindrops pattered down. One missed Dazzle by an antenna-length. She had to keep swerving to avoid getting her wings wet.

"Take shelter under me!" Buster barked to the butterflies. "Fly under my belly — you'll be dry there."

Dazzle didn't need to be told twice. She and Skipper swooped down until they almost brushed the ground, then they ducked beneath Buster's shaggy

fur. "Phew," Dazzle said with a sigh. "I don't like the rain."

"Me, neither," Skipper agreed, fluttering her wings to keep up with Buster.

Lightning flashed and thunder boomed overhead, making both butterflies jump. Buster let out a whine as he ran.

"We're almost there," Skipper called to him. "Head for that black cherry tree."

Buster ran toward the tree, where Mallow and Twinkle were waiting. "Over here!" Dazzle heard Twinkle shout. "This way!"

Buster slowed down when they reached the tree. Dazzle and Skipper flew out from under his belly and

showed him the little cocoon lying on the ground, still wriggling. Thunder growled above them once more, and lightning flashed. In the burst of bright light, Dazzle saw the cocoon crack. The tip of a tiny wing poked through.

"Quickly," she shouted. "There's no time to lose!"

CHAPTER SEVEN

A New Arrival

Without hesitating, Buster bent down and gingerly picked up the cocoon between his jaws.

Dazzle could hardly watch as he carried the cocoon to the tree trunk. His teeth were so sharp. What if he accidentally bit through it?

"Go, Buster!" Mallow cheered.

The rain was
pouring so hard
now that Buster
didn't see a rabbit
hole in the ground.
He stumbled, but
caught himself and
took the last few steps to the tree. He
gently set down the wiggling cocoon and
nudged it inside the hollow. Then he lay
down in front of the entrance to shelter it
from the wind. The baby butterfly was
finally safe from the storm.

Dazzle, Skipper, Twinkle, and
Mallow all flew into the hollow, too. It
was cozy and dry inside, and they could
hear the rain drumming on the ground.

"Thank you, Buster!" Dazzle called,
relieved. They had done it!

"Oh, look!" Twinkle cried. "We were just in time."

The split in the cocoon was growing larger. One crumpled, fragile wing slowly emerged, then another. The new butterfly tentatively put out his legs. "What's happening?" his small voice rang out from inside the cocoon.

"It's all right, keep going!" Dazzle called.

The cocoon fell away from the tiny insect, and he unfolded his wings for the first time.

Dazzle felt more excited than ever before. "Hello," she said softly. "Welcome."

The little butterfly gazed around in wonder and opened his wings fully. Even in the darkness of the hollow, Dazzle could see that they were beautiful, shimmery bluish-purple wings with red and orange spots.

"Oh, aren't you tiny?" she said, watching her small new friend.

The butterfly looked at her with wide eyes. "Is that my name?" he asked. "Is my name Tiny?"

The other butterflies smiled. "If you like," Skipper replied. "I think Tiny is a perfect name for you."

"I'm Dazzle," Dazzle said, "and these are my friends — Skipper, Twinkle, and Mallow. It's so nice to meet you, Tiny."

Tiny gazed around at them all. "Hi," he said shyly. "What's that noise?" he asked.

"It's a storm," Dazzle told him. "We brought you in here to keep you dry. If it wasn't for Skipper's bravery and quick thinking, you might have been stuck out there in the rain."

Tiny smiled at Skipper. "Thank you," he said. "I'm glad you helped me."

"My pleasure," Skipper replied.

Tiny studied his wings, then looked at everyone else's. "Why do we all look so

different?" he wondered aloud. The question reminded Dazzle of her first day as a butterfly. She didn't even know what kind of creature she was at first!

"We're all different types of butterflies," Twinkle explained. She spread her colorful wings proudly. "My beautiful markings show that I'm a peacock butterfly."

"I'm a holly blue," Skipper went on. "Mallow is a cabbage white, and Dazzle's a pale clouded yellow." She peered at Tiny's markings. "I'd say you're a red-spotted purple butterfly."

"That means you're almost as gorgeous as me!" Twinkle said.

Tiny gave his wings a little flap. "Will I be able to fly?" he asked.

Dazzle smiled at him. "Of course," she said, and peeked outside. The rain had stopped. "The storm is over," she told Tiny. "Do you want to try flying now?"

CHAPTER EIGHT

Flying High

"Oh, yes!" Tiny cried, bouncing up and down and flapping his wings. He floated up into the air for a few seconds, and looked surprised. The other butterflies laughed.

"He's a natural!" Mallow giggled. "Come on, Tiny, you're definitely ready

to fly. That's all you have to do — just flap your wings."

"See if you can flutter outside," Skipper suggested.

Tiny flapped his wings energetically . . .

and flew straight into Buster! "Oops," Tiny said, laughing.

Buster gave a friendly bark and got to his feet.

"That's Buster," Dazzle said. "He's the dog that carried you to safety."

"Oh," Tiny said, wide-eyed. "Thank you, Buster."

"You're welcome," Buster replied.

"Buster!" Someone was calling to the

dog. *It sounds like the sheep we met earlier,* Dazzle thought.

Buster gave the butterflies a wink. "I'd better get back," he said. "Those sheep can't get along without me."

As Buster trotted off, the butterflies flew out of the hollow. Now that the storm had passed, other animals were emerging from their shelters, too. Birds chirped overhead, insects scuttled about, and the bunnies hopped up, excited to meet the new butterfly.

"These are bunnies," Twinkle told Tiny as he gazed up at their friendly faces. "They tried their hardest to keep you safe, too."

"Hi," Tiny said. "Thank you all. I'm really lucky to have had so much help on

my first day as a butterfly." Then he
flapped his wings again. "Wheeee!
Look at me!"

"Go, Tiny!" the bunnies cheered.

After a little more practice, Tiny was
able to fly high into the air. The clouds
had drifted away now, and the sun was
shining.

"Let's go back to Butterfly Meadow,"
Twinkle suggested. "Tiny, we can
introduce you to all the other butterflies.
I know you'll like it there."

Tiny did a little loop in the air. "I love
being a butterfly!" he cried happily.

The butterflies said good-bye to the
bunnies and set off for home. As they left

the forest, Dazzle could see raindrops clinging to spiderwebs in the grass.

She glanced back to make sure Tiny was all right. He was keeping up without a problem, flapping his wings and beaming. "I love flying!" he called.

Dazzle smiled at him. *Four butterflies set out exploring today, and now five of us are flying back to Butterfly Meadow,* she thought happily. Their adventures had been scary at times, but look what had happened. They'd found a new butterfly! And even better — they'd made a new friend.

❀ FUN FACTS! ❀
A World of Butterflies

Blue Mormon Monkey Puzzle

Orange Tip   Common Sootywing

Small Postman Painted Lady

Funny names, huh? This could be a list of new cartoon characters, or maybe the names of family pets. But in fact, this is only a short list of the 17,000 types of butterflies found around the world!

Butterflies live on every continent, except Antarctica. Different butterflies live in different parts of the world. For example, the Queen Alexandra's birdwing, the largest and rarest butterfly, is only found in the rain forest of New

Guinea. But the cabbage white is found almost everywhere!

Butterflies come in all colors, shapes, and sizes. The Queen Alexandra's birdwing has wings that stretch ten inches wide. The smallest butterfly — the pygmy blue, found in the southern United States — has tiny wings only a half-inch wide. Butterflies' wing patterns may have stripes, dots, and speckles in all different shades. For example, the green swallowtail's wings are neon green, while the crimson rose's have bright red crescents.

Many different kinds of butterflies have been around for ages. Did you know that butterflies existed even in the time of dinosaurs? Let's hope they are around for many more years!

Dazzle is at home in

Here's a sneak peek at her next
adventure,

Dazzle's
New Friend!

CHAPTER ONE

Fun in the Orchard

"Ready?" Dazzle called excitedly, fluttering her pale yellow wings. "Here we go!"

Dazzle and her butterfly friends, Skipper, Twinkle, and Mallow, were playing in the apple orchard. They'd found a big fallen leaf balanced on the branch of an apple tree, and were using it as a seesaw. Dazzle and Twinkle perched on one side of the leaf, with Skipper and Mallow on the other side. They rocked as fast as they could. Dazzle loved seeing how the bright sunshine filtered through the leaves and made her friends' wings glow. On such a beautiful day, Dazzle didn't have a care in the world.

"Let's bounce even higher, Dazzle!" Twinkle suggested.

The two butterflies flew up into the air, then dove down onto the leaf. The leaf tipped and sent Mallow and Skipper sailing up toward the sky.

"Yay!" Skipper laughed, swooping back down. "This is so much fun!"

"Now it's our turn," Twinkle said eagerly.

This time, Skipper and Mallow flew

up high, then dove down on their side of the leaf. Dazzle and Twinkle soared into the air.

"Wheee!" the two butterflies cried, giggling.

Dazzle couldn't wait to do it again! She was so lucky to have friends like Skipper, Mallow, and Twinkle to play with in the orchard near Butterfly Meadow.

"It's our turn now," Mallow called. But as Dazzle and Twinkle landed on the other side of the leaf, a gruff voice rang through the air.

"Excuse me!"

The four butterflies froze and looked at each other in surprise.

"Who said that?" asked Skipper, looking around the apple tree.

There's magic in every book!

The Rainbow Fairies
Books #1-7

The Weather Fairies
Books #1-7

The Jewel Fairies
Books #1-7

The Pet Fairies
Books #1-7

The Fun Day Fairies
Books #1-7

SCHOLASTIC

www.scholastic.com
www.rainbowmagiconline.com

HIT entertainment

FAIRY3